# MACKINAW CITY MUMMIES

"Johnathan Rand is my favorite author!"
*-Kelly S., age 8, Michigan*

"AMERICAN CHILLERS are great. I got one
for Christmas, and I loved it. Now, my sister
is reading it. When she's done, I'm going to
read it again."
*-Joel F., age 13, New York*

"I like the CHILLERS books because they are
fun to read. They are scary, too."
*-Hannah K., age 11, Minnesota*

"I read the MEGA-MONSTERS book and I
really liked it. Mr. Rand is a great writer."
*-Ryan M., age 12, Arizona*

"I LOVE AMERICAN CHILLERS!"
*-Zachary R., age 8, Indiana*

"I read your book to my little sister and
she got freaked out. I did, too!"
*-Jason J., age 12, Ohio*

"These books are my favorite! I love reading them!"
*-Sarah N., age 10, New Jersey*

"Your books are great. Please write more so I can read them.
*-Dylan H., age 7, Tennessee*

# #10: Mackinaw City Mummies

# An AudioCraft Publishing, Inc. book

No part of this publication may be reproduced in whole or in part, or stored in a retrieval system, or transmitted in any form or by any means, electronic, mechanic, photocopying, recording, or otherwise, without written permission from the publisher. For information regarding permission, write to: AudioCraft Publishing, Inc., PO Box 281, Topinabee Island, MI 49791

Michigan Chillers #10: Mackinaw City Mummies
ISBN 1-893699-18-8

**Librarians/media specialists:**
PCIP/MARC records available at www.americanchillers.com

Cover Illustrations by Dwayne Harris
Cover layout and design by Sue Harring

Printed in USA

# Mackinaw
# City
# Mummies

# VISIT THE OFFICIAL WORLD HEADQUARTERS OF AMERICAN CHILLERS & MICHIGAN CHILLERS!

The all-new HOME for books by Johnathan Rand! Featuring books, hats, shirts, bookmarks and other cool stuff not available anywhere else in the world! Plus, watch the American Chillers website for news of special events and signings at *CHILLERMANIA* with author Johnathan Rand! Located in northern lower Michigan, on I-75 just off exit 313!

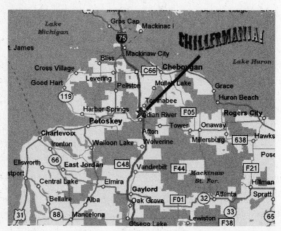

# OPENING OCTOBER, 2005!

www.americanchillers.com

# PART ONE:
# DISCOVERY

The late evening sun was setting fast. The shadows were growing longer, and the air was growing cooler as I traipsed down the dirt trail, carrying a shovel over my shoulder. My dad and I were going fishing in a couple days, and I wanted to find some worms. There's a spot in the woods, not far from our house that is a perfect place to dig for them. Big, fat, juicy night-crawlers. They were the best bait for catching fish.

But tonight, I would be finding more than just nightcrawlers. I would also find a strange object . . . an object that would lead to a terrifying discovery: a big stone tomb, buried in the ground.

That's where I found the mummy. Not some silly, fake mummy that someone made as a joke . . . but a real, honest-to-goodness mummy, sealed in a tomb.

Which was kind of cool, except for one big problem:

The mummy's curse.

Oh, I know what you're thinking. You've probably seen lots of TV shows and movies about mummies, and what happens to people who disturb the tombs. They say that strange things happen. Terrible things.

Well, the legends are *true*. All of them. I know, and it all began the night I went to dig for worms.

By the time I found my favorite worm-hunting spot, the sun had set. Dark shadows crept through the forest, and the creatures of the night began to emerge. I could hear bats flitting through the trees, and crickets singing in the swamp. These are sounds we hear a lot in Mackinaw City, which is where I live. Mackinaw

City is right at the very tip of Michigan's lower peninsula, and I've lived here for all of my eleven years.

I plunged the shovel blade into the soft earth, and brought up a clump of dark dirt, leaving a small black hole in the ground. Then I dumped the contents of the shovel blade next to my foot, and began to sift it with my hands. The dirt was cold and clammy. It was difficult to see in the growing gloom, and I wished I'd remembered my flashlight.

"Good grief, Josh," I scolded myself aloud. "You'd forget your head if it wasn't attached."

That's my name—Josh Patterson. And, while I usually don't talk to myself, I figured that no one was around to hear me. Besides . . . forgetting my flashlight was a pretty dumb move.

Suddenly, I heard twigs and branches snapping. I turned to see what it was.

*Nothing!*

In the murky darkness, it was difficult to make anything out besides the shadowy forms of trees and branches.

I returned to sifting the dirt, and almost immediately found a big, fat nightcrawler. Cool! I dropped him into my jar and sifted through the dirt some more. I found three more crawlers, and then I dug another small hole.

Wow! Four more nightcrawlers! Bonus! But suddenly —

*Snap. Crunch.*

The noise was closer this time! I spun.

*Still nothing!*

After a few seconds, I returned to my work. I plunged the shovel blade into the earth and brought up another clump of dirt.

*Crunnnnch! Snap!*

This time the sound was so close I almost jumped out of my clothes!

I dropped the shovel and spun . . . and I was horrified by what I saw.

# 2

What I saw was no animal, that's for sure. It was tall . . . nearly as tall as me . . . and it was all white. Branches continued to break as it drew closer. It was the shape of a human, arms outstretched. As it approached, it spoke!

"*Josssssshhhh,*" the voice curdled. "*I'm comingggg for yooooouuuuuuu. I'm coming for you, Josh!*"

Terror gripped my body like a wrench. My skin crawled. I grasped the shovel tightly, ready to defend myself.

"I'm warning you!" I screamed. "I have a shovel! Stay away from me! Stay away!"

The white form suddenly stopped. In the sky above, a silver moon slipped in and out of dark clouds.

"Hey, take it easy," a familiar voice croaked. "It was just a joke. Don't be swinging that shovel at me."

I relaxed when I heard the voice, and I leaned closer to the figure, now only a few feet away.

"Robyn?" I asked hesitantly. "Is that you?"

"You bet!" Robyn piped, taking a step toward me. I could see her better now. She was grinning, and the moon above glowed in her eyes.

"It *is* you!" I cried.

"We just got here today," she said. "About an hour ago."

I met Robyn Moore a few years ago. Her family is from Grand Rapids, and they have a summer cottage not far from where we live. During the summer, they come up to Mackinaw City almost every weekend. Sometimes, they stay for a couple weeks.

And she's the *exact* same age as I am! We were both born on the very same day! We get along really well, and we have a lot of fun when she visits.

Clouds swept over the moon, darkening the area around us even more.

"Man! You *really* spooked me!" I said, laughing.

"That was what I wanted to do," she giggled. "I thought you might need a good scare!"

The moon slipped out from behind the clouds, and I could see her better. She was wearing a white shirt and white pants.

"With that outfit," I said, "you look like you could be a ghost."

"Mom wanted me to wear something bright if I was going to be out after dark," she replied.

"How did you find me?" I asked curiously. Not many people know about my favorite worm-hunting spot.

"Your dad told me. He said you guys are going fishing in a few days, and that you were out here digging for worms. I followed the winding footpath until I heard you digging. I wanted to surprise you."

"Well, it worked," I replied, nodding my head. "You surprised me, alright."

"Find any worms?"

"Yeah," I said. I bent down and picked up the jar. "A bunch. Wanna hold one of'em?" I held the jar out.

"Don't be gross," she grimaced, and quickly changed the subject. "Hey . . . you wanna head over to Mackinaw Crossings and get an ice cream cone?"

Mackinaw Crossings is a large, outdoor mall of sorts. It's right downtown, and there are all kinds of shops and stores, and a lot more cool things as well. There are jugglers that wander around, singers and dancers . . . all kinds of really cool stuff. And in the summertime, there's always a ton of people there.

"Sure," I replied. "But I've got to find a few more nightcrawlers first. Why don't I meet you there?"

"Fifteen minutes?" Robyn asked.

"Twenty. I've got to go home and change clothes."

Robyn disappeared down the dark path. Her white form quickly faded from sight, but I could hear the snapping of branches as she made her way through the dark forest. Soon, she was gone.

I raised the shovel and plunged it into the ground. The steel blade suddenly clanged on something hard.

And that's when I saw the flash of silver in the ground. Something was gleaming from the small hole!

Looking back, I wished I would have left it alone. I should have just continued digging, searching for worms.

But I was curious. The silver flash caught my attention, and I wanted to see what it was. So, I knelt down onto the ground to investigate, not knowing that I was about to make a discovery that would lead to one of the most bizarre experiences I've ever had.

Slivers of moonlight whittled through the trees. The silver object flashed, and I reached for it.

It was some kind of symbol. It looked like a cross . . . a cross with a loop on the top of it. The object wasn't very big—maybe three inches long or so.

But it was *heavy*. I was certain that, whatever this strange object was, it must be made of pure silver!

"Wow!" I exclaimed to no one but myself. I held the object in my hand, feeling its weight in my palm. Then I held it up to the moon.

It looked like it was a piece of jewelry of some

sort. It seemed to me that I'd seen something like this before, but I couldn't remember where.

I sifted through the loose dirt to see if there was anything else, but my brief search was fruitless.

*Strange*, I thought. *What's something like this doing way out here? Buried in the ground?*

Whatever it was, I thought it might be valuable. I stuffed the heavy object into my pocket. If I was going to meet Robyn on time, I'd have to get a move on.

Besides . . . I wanted to get home so I could better examine the object I had found.

The trail was dark, but I've traveled it enough times to know it well. I know where it turns, where the mud hole is, and where a small creek flows. I know where the mud wasps have a nest—and I keep away from those nasty buggers.

So, I'm never really worried that I'd ever get lost. Besides—the moon was full tonight. Between clouds, it provided plenty of light to see where I was going.

But when a dark cloud suddenly darkened the sky, I stopped. The cloud had covered the moon so swiftly that it was like someone had turned off a light. I stopped on the trail, turned, and looked up into the night sky — and the awful sight, high above, made me drop both my shovel and my jar of worms.

High in the sky, a dark, billowing cloud had covered the moon.

But it was more than just a cloud.

It was an eye. It was a single, glaring eye, staring down at me. But there was more to it than that. The eye seemed like it was some sort of strange design, like it had been written into the clouds with a magic marker.

I clasped my hands into fists and rubbed my eyes, certain that the bizarre sight above me was some sort of illusion.

Not so. When I lowered my hands, the eye was still there!

It was a nightmare! I refused to believe what I was seeing, yet I was trembling with fear.

I bolted, completely forgetting my shovel and jar of worms. I didn't care if I ever saw them again. I just wanted out of the forest.

My feet raced along the dark, snaking trail. I didn't look over my shoulder. I wouldn't. I couldn't. I was so horrified that I just wanted to forget what was happening.

And when I tripped, I thought that it was the worst thing that could possibly happen.

I was wrong.

Because when I hit the ground, I rolled, and caught a glimpse up at the chilling sight above me.

My heart clanged. My mind spun. My breath was stolen.

*The eye was glowing!* It was glowing like it was on fire! And it was coming closer!

And so, as I lay on the ground, staring up at the incredible sight above, I decided to make a break for it. I had no choice. I knew the trail well, and if I didn't trip again, I was sure I could get away this time.

I was *sure* of it.

I slowly propped myself up on my elbows. The eye glared menacingly down at me, watching, waiting. It was the freakiest thing I'd ever seen.

I sprang up and tore down the trail, my feet thumping on the ground as I ran . . . hoping that I could get away.

It would only take me a few minutes to get out of the woods. I ran as fast as I could, glancing back every few seconds to see if the eye was still there.

It was—until I got out of the forest! When I made it to the edge of the woods, the eye had vanished.

Bizarre. Totally bizarre.

I ran home, changed my clothes, and immediately headed for Mackinaw Crossings. Robyn wasn't going to believe me when I told her what I'd just been through!

I found her near the water fountain, and explained what had happened in the last half-hour.

"Let me see that thing you found," she said, after I'd told her about the curious silver object I'd discovered in the ground.

"Wow," she said. "That's an ankh."

"A what?" I asked.

"It's an ankh," she repeated. "It's an ancient Egyptian symbol. It means 'life'. I learned all about ancient Egypt in my world history class."

"Well, it might mean *'life'* to the ancient Egyptians, but what just happened almost scared me to *death!*"

Robyn peered curiously at the strange, shiny object. "I'd like to go see where you found this thing," she said.

"What?!?!?!" I exclaimed. "Tonight?!?!?! You can't be serious!"

Robyn nodded her head. "Yeah, I am. Let's go check it out."

And for some crazy reason, I said yes. Maybe I felt that if there were two of us, we would be safer.

Maybe.

We walked to my house. I grabbed a

flashlight and left a note for Mom and Dad, just in case they got home before I did. They were at the movies, but they'd be home soon.

We walked back down the street, heading for the edge of town.

"The trail is right here," I said, clicking the flashlight on. Robyn followed me into the forest. I kept looking up into the sky to see if the mysterious eye had appeared, but it wasn't there.

"Are you sure you're just not making all of this up?" Robyn asked.

"No!" I insisted. "I'm not making this up!"

"Well, I don't see anything weird," she said.

But no sooner had she spoke when a strange, misty form appeared in the darkness. It was on the path in front of us — and it was coming closer!

I grasped Robyn's arm, then froze.

"Do . . . do you see that?" I whispered.

"Yes!" she replied. "What is it?"

"I don't know," I answered, my voice trembling. "It could be anything. I've seen some pretty strange things tonight."

We stood on the trail, surrounded by dark shadows. The milky-white form kept coming toward us.

"Do you think it's a ghost?" Robyn asked quietly. Her voice trembled a bit, too, and I was glad that I wasn't the only one that was a little scared.

"I have no idea," I whispered. "It could be anything!"

The mysterious form drew closer and closer.

"Josh," Robyn said after a few moments. "It looks like . . . like . . . ."

"A mummy!" I finished. "It is! It's a mummy!"

We were more than just afraid. We were horrified.

The mummy slowly lurched toward us, and with every step, we could see him clearer. It was a human form, wrapped in creamy-white bandages. His eye sockets were dark, black holes, and the creature's arms were outstretched, as if reaching for us.

And then: it spoke!

"Aaaaaaannnnnnnnnkkkkkkhhhhh," the mummy moaned. Its voice was low and very gruff, and sounded hollow-like. It was really eerie. "Aaaaaaaaaaannnnnkkkkhhhh," it repeated.

"It wants the ankh you found!" Robyn said. "Give it to him!"

"What?!?!" I exclaimed, taking a step back. "Are you kidding?!?!? I'm not going near that thing!!"

The mummy kept coming. In a few seconds, he would reach us.

"I've got a better idea," I said.

"What?"

"Let's run!"

We fled. It only took us a few seconds to reach the edge of the forest. We both looked back.

No mummy. Whew.

"We've got to come back here and find out what's going on," Robyn said, her breath heaving. We had both sprinted pretty fast, and we gasped for air.

"Fine with me," I said. "But let's wait until tomorrow, when it's daylight. I don't want to come back here in the dark. Besides . . . I've got to go back there to get my shovel and my jar of worms. It would be hard to find them in the dark."

We agreed to meet at my house in the morning and make plans from there. I walked Robyn to her summer house, said good-night, and walked home . . . completely unaware of the terror we would experience the very next day.

# 7

Robyn met me at my house at nine the next morning. She rode her bicycle, but she decided to leave it at my house. We could walk to the forest since it wasn't far away.

When we made it to the edge of the woods, we stopped. I scanned the sky searching for the eye, but it wasn't there. And we didn't see any mummies, either.

"Come on," I said, taking a step onto the trail. "Let's go see if we can find more of these shiny things."

"You mean 'ankh', Robyn replied.

"Whatever. I'd like to find more. Maybe it's

worth a lot of money."

"It's probably just something that someone bought in a gift store," Robyn mused. "They probably lost it."

We came to the place on the trail where I'd left my shovel. I picked it up. The jar of worms was only a few feet away, and I was glad that it hadn't broken. All of my worms seemed fine.

Finally, after a few more minutes of walking, we came to the place where I had been digging the night before. I drove the blade into the soft ground and removed a small amount of dirt.

"Nothing here," she said, peering at the small mound of soil clumped on the blade. I sank the shovel into the ground again. And again. We found nothing. I dug for a few minutes, then tried another spot.

Still nothing.

"Are you sure we're in the right place?" Robyn asked.

"I'm positive," I answered. "This is where I always come to dig for worms. This is the place where I found that thing last night."

"Maybe there aren't any more," Robyn said in

disappointment.

"Maybe. But we'll try a few more times."

I hastily drove the shovel into the ground again. This time, it clanged heavily on something. Something solid, and big enough to stop the blade.

There was something there.

"Criminy," I said. "That rock must be huge. I pulled the blade from the ground, and we looked into the small, shallow hole.

The object wasn't a rock at all, but a flat slab of gray cement. It seemed too uniform and cultured to be an ordinary rock.

"Dig around it!" Robyn whispered excitedly. "It might be something!"

"Well, of course it's something," I said smartly. *"Everything* is *something."*

She ignored me, and knelt closer to the hole I was digging.

"Stop!" she suddenly cried. Her hands

brushed frantically over the stone. "Josh! Look at this!"

I put the shovel down and kneeled into the soft earth. The light glowed in the hole, and Robyn was reaching down, quickly brushing dirt from the partially uncovered slab.

"There's writing on this!" Robyn said excitedly. "It's some sort of strange lettering!"

I peered closer.

Robyn was right! There was some sort of odd markings on the slab of stone.

"I can't read any of it," Robyn said. "It looks like there are just a bunch of weird symbols. They might be Egyptian symbols, like the ankh you found. Dig some more."

I stood up and began digging around the hole, careful not to slam the blade into the hard slab. Soon, I had cleared away a larger area.

"Okay," Robyn said. "Let's see what we've got."

Again, I set down the shovel and dropped to my knees. We swept our hands over the smooth surface, brushing away small clumps of dirt. Soon, we had dug up all around it. The stone was big; bigger than we were. There was no way we would be able to move it.

And the writing on the stone wasn't really writing like English letters or anything. The writing was just a bunch of Egyptian symbols . . . strange symbols that I didn't understand.

"What do you think it is?" Robyn asked, her voice filled with wonder.

"I don't know," I replied, shaking my head in the darkness. "I don't have a clue."

"These markings might be hieroglyphics."

"Hiero-*what?*" I asked.

"Hi-row-GLIF-icks," she repeated slowly.

"Hieroglyphics?" I said correctly, and she nodded.

"Hieroglyphics," she said again. "You know. Like what the ancient Egyptians used. Pictures drawn to tell a story."

"Oh, yeah," I said. "I guess I've heard of those before." I paused. "But . . . what are they doing here? In Mackinaw City?"

"You've got me," she shrugged. "I don't have a clue."

We were excited with our find. What could it

be? What did it mean? And why was something like this buried in the woods near Mackinaw City?

It didn't make sense.

"Josh," Robyn suddenly whispered, pointing up into the sky. "Look up there!"

I tilted my head back and gazed up. Puffy white clouds hung beneath a blue canopy.

*The eye had returned!* A big, wide eye, staring down at us from the clouds!

"That's what I saw last night!" I said. "That's it! That's the eye!"

*"Holy cow!"* Robyn whispered.

But then something else happened.

"Robyn," I said quietly. "Look down."

She looked down at the gray slab exposed beneath our feet.

*The same, curious symbol that lit up the night sky was now glowing on the stone!* Right at our feet, the eye on the stone slab glowed neon-white, brighter than the sun! It seemed to pulsate every few seconds, glowing brighter, then dimmer, brighter, then dimmer.

I looked up at the strange sight in the sky,

then back down at the slab of cement again. Up, then down.

A cold wind seemed to swish right through me, although there was no breeze. Robyn felt the cold, too, and she shivered.

Until now, things had been strange. Finding the odd silver object while digging for worms, the eye in the sky, the vanishing mummy, and now the stone in the ground.

What did it all mean?

As strange as it seems, it would all make sense later. Things were about to go from strange — to all out crazy. Call it a nightmare, call it whatever you want . . . it doesn't matter.

Because what would happen later that afternoon would change my life — and Robyn's — *forever*.

# PART TWO: THE EYE IN THE SKY

# 9

Suddenly the eye in the sky vanished. The eye on the stone stopped glowing.

"What was that all about?" I asked.

"You've got me," Robyn said. "That was too freaky."

What did it all mean? How did that huge stone get in the ground? And when? Was there something beneath it? Inside it?

"Let's go down to the library," Robyn suggested. "I'll bet they have some books on this kind of stuff."

I shook my head. "You'll have to go alone," I

said. "Dad wants me to mow the lawn today."

We left the strange place. Both of us kept looking around, wondering what kind of weird thing would happen next. Thankfully, nothing strange happened on our way home.

• • •

I had just finished cutting the grass, and I was putting the mower away when Robyn showed up, carrying an armload of books.

"I found these at the library," she explained. "They're all about mummies and ancient Egyptian symbols. Wait 'till you see what I've found!" She sat down on the ground, and placed the pile of books next to her. I sat cross-legged in the grass as she opened up one of the larger books.

The wind howled at our ears, and gray clouds tumbled in the sky above. A storm was coming in, and it was supposed to rain soon. Trees groaned and howled, their limbs tossed about by the heavy gusts.

"There were a bunch of books about

mummies and things," Robyn said, her eyes scanning the pages. "But this book was by far the most interesting."

"Wait a minute," I said, glancing at the pages. "That's not a book about mummies. That's a book about Mackinaw City."

"Right," Robyn agreed. "When I asked the librarian if they had any books on mummies, she showed me a bunch. But she also found this one. It's an old history book about Mackinaw City."

I still wasn't following her. What would an old Mackinaw City history book have to do with the strange stone we'd found in the forest?

"There is a legend from a long time ago," Robyn began. "Way back during the war. Back when Fort Michilimackinac was built."

I knew all about the fort. It's really old, and if you ever go to Mackinaw City, you can actually visit the old structure. They have re-enactments and activities there all summer. Actually, it's a pretty cool place.

A gust of wind threw our hair about. Robyn pulled a lock away from her face, and continued speaking.

"A long time ago, an Egyptian ship was said to have sailed the world, looking for the sacred Caves of Monkammen."

"The Caves of Monkammen?" I said in disbelief. I've heard of the old caves. Ancient Egyptians believed that there were caves that stretched beneath their great pyramids in Egypt. The caves were supposed to wind all the way through the entire earth. The Straits of Mackinac—where Lake Michigan and Lake Huron come togther—was thought to be the place where the entrance was on this side of the world. Somewhere in Mackinaw City, some believe, is the entrance to the Caves of Monkammen.

But not many people, of course, believe in such a thing. It's just an old wives' tale.

"The Egyptians landed here, in what is now Mackinaw City," Robyn continued. "The legend is that they found the entrance to the caves of Monkammen . . . but they didn't find what they thought they would."

"This sounds like something from a mystery book or movie," I said in disbelief.

"I know," Robyn agreed, nodding her head.

A raindrop hit me in the face, then another. A heavy drop smacked a page in the open book on Robyn's lap.

"Come on," I urged, leaping to my feet. "Let's go inside before it starts to pour."

We retreated to the garage, and made it just in time. The sky opened up, and the rain came down in buckets. Robyn and I sat on two lawn chairs in the garage, watching the downpour.

"Anyway," she began again, flipping the book open, "here's the really weird part. All of the Egyptians returned to Egypt."

Robyn stopped speaking and looked at me.

"That's it?" I asked. "So what? They didn't find what they were looking for, and they went back home. What's the big deal?"

"The big deal," Robyn answered, "is that the ship was left *here*. In Mackinaw City."

Suddenly, I knew what she was getting at! If the ship had sank in Mackinaw, that would mean that the Egyptians found another way to make it back to Egypt!

"They must have found the caves!" I exclaimed. "The caves must really exist!"

Robyn nodded excitedly. "It's all right here!" she said, her voice rising with elation. "But look at this. This is what's really crazy. A long time ago, a man was clearing the forest to build a house. But he found something. Something in the forest. Whatever he found, whatever happened to him, he didn't say. He gathered up his family that day, and they left. They didn't take any of their belongings. Nothing. They just left."

"That's freaky," I said.

"It gets better," Robyn continued. "That night, many people in the town reported seeing something very strange in the sky. An artist from the paper drew a picture of what was spotted."

Robyn turned the page to show me the drawing in the book—and I just about fell out of my chair.

I gasped.

Robyn turned and smiled, proud of what she'd discovered. She handed the book to me for a closer look.

*It was the eye!* The same eye that we'd seen in the sky last night! The same eye that had glowed brightly on the stone slab!

"But . . . but . . . ." I stammered. "How could—"

Robyn was shaking her head. "Beats me," she said. "But there it is. The same thing that they saw, years ago, was the same thing that we saw, last night."

Talk about being freaked out! I stared at the drawing in the old book. Outside the garage, the rain fell and the wind blew. The sky was dark and gray.

"We have to go and find what's out there," I whispered softly.

"Huh?" Robyn replied. I'd spoken so quietly that she hadn't heard me.

"We have to find out what's buried in the ground," I repeated, turning to face her.

She grinned. "I was hoping you'd say that," she stated. "I'm more curious than ever to find out just what all of this means."

I think that, although we were both very excited to find out just what the strange stone was all about, we were both a bit frightened.

After all—what had the man and his family seen that had made them leave for good? What would happen if we saw the same thing?

We spent the next hour flipping through the books that Robyn had borrowed from the library. We found out a lot of interesting things about mummies, pyramids, Egypt, and things like that.

The rain finally stopped. The wind died

down, but the gray clouds remained, warning of more rain.

"Want to head out?" I asked Robyn.

"Yeah," I said, nodding my head.

Without a word, Robyn folded up the book in her lap and tucked it under her arm. We stood up, picked up our shovels, and set off to begin our dig.

We walked across the street, over a small field, and stopped at the edge of the forest.

"Josh!" Robyn suddenly cried out. "Look!"

I turned my gaze upward and gasped in disbelief.

Dark clouds were tossing in the air, rolling and tumbling about in a strange, swirling shape.

But it was something I had seen before. I recognized the shape instantly.

I gasped, drawing in a long, deep breath.

The eye in the sky had returned.

"Still want to go?" I asked. My mind was spinning and my imagination whirled.

Robyn hesitated a moment, looking up at the mysterious eye, then at me. Finally, she nodded and spoke.

"We have to find out what's going on," she said softly.

Slowly, we started down the trail, with the giant eye looming over us.

We entered the forest, and followed the path deep into the woods. Every few seconds I glanced up to see the strange eye in the sky peering down at us, watching as we wound our way through the thick brush. The smell of cedar and pine drifted into my nose. Droplets of water trickled off branches and leaves, every so often hitting my shoulder or my head. No birds sang. The forest was strangely silent.

Finally, we came upon the spot where we'd been digging the night before.

At first, I was afraid that the stone wouldn't be there at all. Weird things had been happening, and I had wondered if we'd only imagined the stone.

Not so.

As we approached the spot, I could see the piles of dirt that we'd made from digging. When we approached the hole, the gray stone was clearly visible. The markings inscribed in the rock were easy to see in the day, even though the sky was overcast and gray.

And above us, the mysterious eye in the sky continued to peer down at us, watching. It was really weird.

"Hey!" Robyn exclaimed, grabbing my arm. We stopped. "Josh . . . *look!*" She pointed at the stone.

*It had moved!* Somehow, the huge stone slab had moved overnight, and it was placed several feet from where it had been when we left it!

"What in the world is going on?" I wondered aloud.

We approached cautiously . . . and received another surprise — and this one blew me away.

*There were stone steps leading down into the ground!*

"Holy smokes!" I said. "It's some kind of tunnel or cave or something!"

"It's the lost caves of Monkammen!" Robyn whispered. "It has to be!"

It was incredible. The giant rock had covered the stairway for hundreds — maybe thousands — of years.

Now it was open, and I'll give you one guess what we were about to do.

"Are you thinking what I'm thinking?" Robyn asked quietly. All I could do was nod my head. I really wanted to know where those stone steps went.

"I'll go first," I offered taking a step forward.

"Huh-uh," Robyn said, taking a step next to me. "We'll both go together."

And with that, we both took a step down. And another. Then another.

The deeper we went into the cave, the darker it became. I wished that I would have brought my flashlight.

But suddenly, the steps stopped, and we found ourselves in what appeared to be a large room.

*It was a tomb!*

The room was filled with golden urns and silver vases. Shiny chests and boxes were neatly arranged alongside one another. Hieroglyphs, written in black lettering, covered the inside walls of the tomb. There must be millions of dollars worth of gold and silver in this place.

And as our eyes grew accustomed to the dark, I realized that there was something else here.

Something . . . that was *alive*.

A sudden motion had caught my attention. I turned my head.

"*Robyn!*" I whispered. She looked at me, then turned to look at what I was seeing. I heard her gasp in amazement.

On the other side of the tomb, a strange, creamy mist was forming. It grew thicker and thicker as we watched, and it didn't take long to figure out what it was.

It was a *mummy!* Just like the one we'd spotted last night in the forest!

He was a chalky-gray color. His bandages were tattered and torn and looked like they were probably very old. One arm was stretched out, as if the creature was reaching for us.

And another thing that was strange—the mummy seemed *transparent!* It seemed that we could actually see right through him, like he was some kind of ghost-mummy!

*"You're seeing a mummy, too, aren't you?"* I asked Robyn quietly.

*"No, I'm seeing Britney Spears,"* Robyn hissed sarcastically. *"Of course I'm seeing a mummy! But . . . he's not real, is he? He's just like the mummy we saw the other night! The one that just disappeared right in front of us!"*

Suddenly, the mummy began to speak! Bandages around his mouth began to separate as he began to moan.

*"AAAAANNNNKKKKHHHHH,"* the mummy groaned. *"AAAAANNNKKKHHHHH."*

*"He wants that thing I found!"* I whispered, digging my hand into my pocket. I pulled out the ankh. "He wants my ankh!"

Suddenly, without warning, the ankh was pulled from my hand! I tried to grab it, but it was too late. It floated up into the air, and began drifting toward the ghostly mummy. I reached for it and tried to grab it, but it was already out of my reach.

"*AAAAAAANNNKKKHHHH!*" The mummy moaned again, only louder this time.

"I can't believe I'm seeing this!" Robyn exclaimed.

"Me neither!" I replied.

I didn't know what to do. I was horrified, but I didn't think I could run if I tried. I stood my ground, watching the ankh float weightlessly through the air toward the mummy.

"*AAAAAANNNKKKKHHHHH!*" the mummy moaned. His hands were outstretched, reaching for the object. His voice had changed in pitch, and the mummy seemed more excited, more elated as the ankh floated gently in the air. Finally, the silver object drifted close enough for the strange creature to reach out and grasp it in his cloth-wrapped hands!

Suddenly, the cave began to tremble and shake. "What's happening??!?" Robyn yelled over the rumbling.

The mummy was *changing!* Right before our

eyes, the mummy was unraveling! The old, graying bandage strips were falling away. Some of the pieces fell to the ground, and smaller pieces were cast about in the gusting wind.

And the *voice!*

The mummy's voice was no longer a moan. It was a deep, scary laugh that boomed over the fierce storm. The mummy's laugh rose and fell like the blustery gale . . . until he was no longer a mummy at all!

# 13

He was a *man!* A dark haired man, wearing brightly-colored robes, stood where the mummy once was. He had silver and gold rings on his fingers, gold bracelets around his arms, and a gold crown with a single ruby stone on the front. His eyebrows angled sharply over piercing black eyes.

"Two thousand years!" the man suddenly boomed. His voice was throaty and hoarse. "Two thousand years, and the curse has been broken! It was written that I would return, and now . . . I HAVE!!"

He thrust a powerful fist into the air and all

around us the cave trembled.

"Now, I shall have EVERYTHING! Everything I see will be mine!" He laughed a sinister, terrible laugh that snarled like thunder.

Suddenly, the mysterious man spread his arms wide . . . and began sinking into the ground! It was as if the ground was swallowing him up, swallowing him alive. The whole time, he was staring at us with an awful, evil grin.

Robyn remained at my side, shaking. Something terrible had happened. Something awful and wicked and bad. I knew that somehow, someway, we had done something very, very, wrong.

"Let's get out of here," Robyn said, her voice shaking with fear.

We turned to dash up the steps but we were stopped dead in our tracks. There was another loud rumbling. Suddenly, a slab of rock slid in front of the stairs! It happened so quickly that there was nothing we could do. The rock door slid shut, sealing us in the tomb.

We were in total darkness—and we were trapped!

# PART THREE: THE TOMB

Robyn screamed. I screamed. It was so dark we couldn't see our noses in front of our faces.

"How are we going to get out of here?" Robyn cried.

I was worried, too. No one knew that we were here. We could be trapped overnight . . . or longer.

And what if that weird mummy came back? What then?

I placed my hand on the stone door, searching for something to grasp. I found nothing. The rock was too smooth. The only thing I could feel were the grooves of the carved hieroglyphs.

There was noting to grab on to, nothing to grip.

I tried pushing the door. Hah. Good luck. The thing didn't budge a fraction of an inch.

As the minutes passed, I began to grow frantic. I was sure that the tomb was solid . . . and that meant that no air could get in or out. Soon, we would run out of air. Soon, we wouldn't be able to breathe. Slowly, it would become harder and harder to draw even the smallest breath of air. Soon—

*Stop it*, I mentally scolded myself. *Thinking like that isn't going to get us out of here.*

I calmed myself, and assessed our situation. Things really didn't look good. Already, I could feel my lungs beginning to tighten. Breathing was becoming more difficult as our air supply dwindled rapidly.

I was almost ready to give up, to admit defeat—when we saw the glowing eye on the wall of the tomb.

One hieroglyph, an eye, like the one we saw in the sky and on the top of the tomb — was *glowing!* It was glowing, just like we'd seen last night!

I stumbled in the darkness, bumping into heavy objects. My eyes never left the glowing emblem on the wall of the tomb.

It was radiating a brilliant, neon green. The intensity of the light pulsated, growing stronger, then weaker, brighter, then dim.

I found myself wondering if all of this were really happening. I seemed to be in a place where magic and reality collided, and I wasn't sure which was which. What did the glowing eye on the wall mean?

Slowly, I reached up with my finger and placed my hand upon the beaming image.

*It stopped glowing!* I felt a little bit of a shock when the strange, glowing symbol blinked out. But what's more, the ground beneath us began to rumble! From behind us, light suddenly appeared.

*The door was opening!*

I let out a huge sigh of relief, and took a long, deep breath, as fresh air flowed into the tomb. The sweet scent of cedars and pines tickled my nose.

Saved.

"I'm not sure what just happened," I breathed, hastily stepping out of the tomb and into the afternoon daylight. "But I'm glad that thing opened up."

Robyn didn't answer.

"Come on," I said, turning to face her.

But Robyn was gone! She had vanished!

"Robyn!" I called out. My voice echoed through the underground chambers. "Robyn?!?! Come on . . . cut the jokes!"

No answer.

I was getting worried. The tomb had several passageways where she could have gone—but why? Was this just another one of her pranks?

*No, this isn't a prank,* I thought.

Suddenly a shadow appeared behind me. Thank goodness. She wasn't gone after all.

I turned. "How did you—"

My voice froze. I couldn't finish my sentence.

Standing on the stone steps was not Robyn at all. It was a mummy . . . and somehow I knew that I wouldn't escape from this one.

He was hideous. Dusty cloth strips wrapped around his body like linen snakes. Some of the strips were torn and they hung loose, dangling from his body. His entire head was wound with strips, his nose was covered, and there was only a slight opening for his mouth. And his mouth was moving, like he was trying to say something, only no sound came out.

And his *eyes.*

There were two dark openings for his eyes, and when I took a closer look I saw two shiny orbs in those black sockets. I knew that mummies were supposed to be dead, but his eyes looked alive. He could see me. I was certain. He was looking right at me.

The mummy came down the steps, his arms reaching for me. I took a step back, then another, then another.

The mummy took another step down.

Enough was enough. I decided the only way I was going to be able to get away was to make a break for it. I'd have to try and duck beneath the mummy and make a dash up the steps.

I sprang and ducked down as I ran past the mummy. I actually touched him! I could feel the dry cloth wraps touch my skin, and I cringed.

But the mummy didn't seem to pay any attention to me! I thought for sure he would try and grab me as I ran by, but he didn't. He was focused on something on the other side of the tomb.

I stopped at the opening of the tomb, staring back down the stairs. My heart was beating a mile a minute. I watched the mummy as he slowly stumbled to the other side of the small room.

Then I saw what he wanted!

On the other side of the tomb was a long, bronze sword. He reached for it, and, with great difficulty, picked it up.

And what was about to happen was something that I would never forget in a million years.

The mummy began to change! His entire form began to swirl about, just like we had seen before! In seconds, he was no longer a mummy. He looked like an Egyptian warrior!

An Egyptian warrior . . . with a *sword*.

Enough was enough. I was in way over my head. Robyn was missing, and it was time to go for help.

I spun on my heels and began to run as fast as I could. I would run straight home and get Mom and Dad. They would know what to do.

Without warning, I was suddenly seized by what could only be described as an invisible vice.

Something caused me to halt so suddenly that it felt like I had slammed into a brick wall! I came to a sudden stop, and I felt dazed and dizzy. Like I had spun around in circles for too long.

My breath was stolen, and I gasped for air. I grabbed my throat, choking, and struggled to take a deep, long, breath.

And in the next instant, I couldn't move at all! My hands froze around my neck, and one leg froze in mid-stride! And what was really freaky was that I was leaning sideways, off balance. I should have fallen—but my body remained completely motionless!

It was the freakiest—and *weirdest*—feeling I had ever had in my life. I felt helpless, and I was powerless to do anything.

Then: footsteps. I could hear footsteps approaching, but I couldn't turn to face the sound.

But I knew who—or what—was making them.

The man I had spotted in the tomb. I could hear his footsteps as he approached.

I struggled to turn, but it was useless.

*Closer.*

Crunch. Crunch. Crunch. His footsteps were slow and methodical. He knew I couldn't get away.

*Closer . . . .*

I was still struggling when I felt a cold hand on my shoulder. A shadow came over me, and out of the corner of my eye I saw movement.

Suddenly, I could move! I began to fall, but I caught myself by placing my raised foot to the ground. I stumbled, then I stood up, and turned to face the strange man.

And that's when the sword came down. It was raised high above my head, but in one swift motion the freaky Egyptian warrior brought it down . . . and there was no way I would have time to do anything.

I tried to jump back, but I knew that it would be too late.

And it was. Before I even moved an inch, the shiny blade came down, down, down—and plunged into the ground right in front of my feet!

*"Yaaaaahhhh!"* I screamed. I took a giant step back from the man. He was still holding the sword, its blade stuck into the ground.

"You like my magic, no?" he asked. His voice was raspy and deep. His huge, marble-like eyes glared sharply, cutting right through me. His skin was dark, and his hair and beard were jet black.

I took another step back. I thought that maybe, if I could put a little more distance between us, I might try to run again.

He immediately took another step forward, pulling the sword from the ground and letting the blade hang by his side.

"Ah," he said with a sly smile. "A quiet one. But you are impressed, yes?"

I don't know if you could say that I was impressed, but I managed to nod my head.

"Yes, you are impressed," he said. He chuckled, and his eyes burned into mine. "Too bad your friend isn't here to see my magic."

*Robyn!?!?!?*

"What have you done to her!?!?!?!" I demanded sharply. I was sure something terrible had happened. "Where is Robyn?!?!?!"

The strange man turned and looked back at the tomb in the ground. "I'm afraid," he said, "that she has been taken by Akbar the Terrible."

"Ak-who?" I asked.

"Akbar the Terrible," he repeated. "The most powerful name in all the land. Surely you must know of him."

I shook my head from side to side. I'd never heard of anyone by that name.

"What are you talking about?" I asked. My mind was awhirl with confusion and fear.

*Where was Robyn?*

"First, my young friend," he said thickly, "first you must know that I wish you no harm. I have not harmed your friend, and I will not harm you.

"Your friend is safe, but she is in great danger. She has been taken to a place where no mortal should go." His voice was heavy and serious. "Your friend has been taken to Akbar's lair in the lost caves of Monkammen."

My face felt numb, and I couldn't speak. I remembered the story from Robyn's library book. About the caves and tunnels that traveled through the earth, all the way to the other side of the world.

"But that's just a story," I managed to say, shaking my head. "It's not true. It's only a legend."

The man looked at me, and I looked at him. The gray sky reflected in his dark, glossy eyes.

He really was a little out of place with his gold and silver jewelry and colorful clothing. He looked like someone who belonged on the TV screen.

And he looked a little sad. There was a certain sadness in his eyes that told me what he was saying was true.

And it worried me.

But when he explained what was going to happen to Robyn, I wasn't just worried.

I was *horrified.*

"Come. I will explain."

It was all he said. He motioned for me to follow, then turned and began walking toward the unearthed tomb.

"I must thank you for what you have done," he said, walking ahead of me.

"Just what did I do?" I asked.

"You have broken the spell," he replied. "When you found the ankh, you broke the spell. However, in doing so, you have unleashed the curse."

I didn't like the sound of that at all.

"Hey, I was just digging for worms,

Mister . . . Mister —"

"I am called Rhaman. I am one twin of the spirits of King Monkammen."

*Huh?* I thought.

The strange man stopped at the tomb and looked down. I stopped a few feet from him, not wanting to get too close. "Where is Robyn?" I demanded.

Rhaman raised his arm and pointed down into the tomb.

I didn't understand.

"Where is she?" I asked again.

"Look. See." Rhaman waved his finger at the tomb.

"You've got to tell me just what is going on here," I said. "This is all too freaky. Is Robyn in danger? Is she all right?"

Rhaman nodded. "She is in more danger than you know. She has been captured by Akbar the Terrible, and he is going to mummify her."

*Oh no! Robyn was going to be turned into a mummy!*

Rhaman began to explain what had happened, and that's when things began to make sense.  Oh, sure, what was going on was pretty freaky — but it all began to make sense in a strange way.

But when Rhaman told me what I was going to have to do to save Robyn, I became paralyzed with fear.

# 20

Rhaman spoke for over an hour. All the while I listened intently to his bizarre story.

He explained that he was one of two 'spirit twins' of the great King Monkammen, an Egyptian king that lived 2,000 years ago. He was one of the persons on the boat that traveled to Mackinaw City. However, he fell ill and died before he could return. He was mummified, and buried in a tomb . . . the very tomb that we found. From there, King Monkammen's two spirit warriors — Rhaman and Akbar — would guard the entrance to the sacred caves of Monkammen.

"But . . . but that would mean that he's your

brother," I said.

Rhaman nodded. "Yes, it is true. Akbar is my spirit brother. Why he decided to leave the path of good is a mystery to me. We have everything we could ever want or need, but it was not enough for him."

Rhaman told me that Akbar decided that he did not want to guard the caves, and set out on his own. He gathered together thousands of mummies buried in the caves, and brought them to life with his strange magic. He vowed to one day take over the ancient pyramids of the underworld. But Akbar could not succeed because he needed two very powerful symbols: the ankh and the shen.

"You mean the ankh that I found?" I asked. "Was that Akbar that took the ankh from me?" Rhaman nodded.

"Yes, indeed," he affirmed. "The ankh is the ancient Egyptian symbol for life, and it has mystical powers. The shen is the Egyptian symbol for 'eternity'. Akbar the Terrible needs both—the ankh and the shen—and he'll have everything he needs to take over all kingdoms.

The lands below ground, and the land above. Even at this very moment, Akbar is gathering his mummy-slaves in preparation. Now that he has the ankh, all he needs is the shen. The shen is made of gold, and it is about the same size as the ankh. It is a circle with a single bar under it. It is the only thing that Akbar needs. Once he has it, he will be unstoppable."

"Why don't *you* go and get him?" I asked. "You said yourself that you can do magic."

"Akbar tricked me. When I wandered outside the tomb, he closed the door. I've been wandering this place you call Mackinaw City for the past thousand years. I was not allowed to return to the tomb until now — until you found the ankh.

"Come, and I will show you something," Rhaman continued. He walked over to the dimly lit tomb, and I followed him down the dark stone steps.

Inside the tomb he found a small box. Rhaman opened it. Inside was a small crystal pyramid, about the size of a bowling ball. It looked just like one of those giant pyramids in

Egypt, only a lot smaller, of course. It was really cool looking.

"The Stone of Titan," Rhaman explained, holding the glass pyramid into the air. "This will give us a glimpse into the world of Akbar the Terrible."

"How does it work?" I asked.

He held the pyramid in one hand, then waved his other hand above it.

And what I saw was one of the most amazing things I had ever witnessed in my life.

# 21

Instantly, a faint image appeared in the glass! It was cloudy at first, but after a few moments, I could make out vague shapes. It was like looking into some sort of crystal ball.

And the first thing I saw was—

*Mummies!* I could see them walking around inside the pyramid.

But wait! They weren't in the pyramid at all! *They were in Mackinaw City!* In the pyramid, I could see what was going on downtown. I could see cars and people and stores and boats in the water . . . and there were mummies everywhere!

"No one can see them," Rhaman explained.

"Not yet. Not until Akbar finds the shen. When he has the shen, he has promised all of the mummies that they will rule the world with him. And then," Rhaman said sadly, "then all the people of your world will be his slaves. He will force them to build great pyramids, much bigger than the world has ever seen."

He waved his hand over the pyramid, and the scene inside the strange crystal object changed. And what I saw was shocking.

*Robyn!*

But I could tell right away she was in a lot of trouble.

# 22

The scene inside the glass pyramid was horrifying. I saw what seemed to be some sort of dark room. Torches were lit and affixed to the walls.

Robyn was chained to a rock wall. She was struggling to get away, but there were the creatures — mummies — that made sure she couldn't escape. All the while, Akbar the Terrible looked on, laughing devilishly.

"What's he doing?" I asked Rhaman.

"I'm afraid he is going to mummify her," Rhaman answered somberly. "This is the first step."

*A mummy? Robyn?!?! Oh no!*

"Quickly!" Rhaman commanded. "You must act fast! There still might be time to save her if you hurry!"

"*Me?*" I gasped. "Alone? By myself?"

"Because of my very nature, I cannot travel beyond this burial area. I am very powerful here in the tomb, but that is where my magic ends. You must go. If your friend is to be saved, it will be up to you. If Akbar is going to be stopped, you will have to do it."

"But . . . but how?" I asked. "What do I do?"

Rhaman slowly pointed down the dark steps that disappeared into the ground. "You must go," he said solemnly. "You must enter the caves of Monkammen. You must find Akbar . . . and destroy him. You must destroy him before he finds the shen. Before your friend becomes a—"

He didn't have to finish his sentence. I knew exactly what he meant.

Oh, I was afraid, alright. A million questions spun through my head. There was no way I'd have answers for all of them.

Not now, anyway.

Right now, the important thing was Robyn. She was in great danger, and every second that I spent worrying about it was a second wasted.

"I'll go," I said bravely.

And that's when things *really* got freaky.

# PART FOUR: THE CAVES

# 23

"Take this," Rhaman commanded. He handed me the crystal pyramid. "This will guide you to your friend. But it will also lead you to Akbar."

I rolled the pyramid over in my hands. It was heavy, and it was all shiny and smooth.

"But what about the shen?" I asked. "Where is it?"

"When the time comes, you will know," Rhaman answered. "When the time comes."

Then Rhaman reached into a small vase-like container. He dipped his finger in and brought it back out. The tip of his finger was covered with a dark oil. Rhaman reached out and put his finger to my forehead. "Hold still."

"What are you doing?"

"You'll see. Hold still."

He dragged his finger across my forehead, made a few swirls and whirls, then pulled his hand away.

"The Eye of Horus," he explained.

I looked into the crystal pyramid, and I could see my reflection.

*It was the same, weird eye that I'd seen in the sky! The same eye that had been glowing on the tomb!*

"The Eye of Horus is an ancient symbol for protection," Rhaman continued. "It will give you some defense against Akbar's wicked power."

"Huh?" I asked. "Wicked power?"

Rhaman was about to speak, when all of a sudden the pyramid came to life. A fine mist began swirling about in the object, and then shapes began to form. As they became clearer, I could make out figures and forms moving about.

*Mummies!*

There were mummies sluggishly walking about in a darkened cave. They were leading someone somewhere, and that someone was in chains.

And I knew that someone was Robyn.

"You must go!" Rhaman shouted. "Now! Quickly!"

"But . . . but—" I still had a lot of questions, but it didn't look like I would be getting any answers.

"Just remember," Rhaman said, "much of what you will see is not real. The Eye of Horus will protect you, and the Stone of Titan will guide you." Rhaman suddenly grasped my shoulders and thrust me into the tomb. Immediately, I was racing down the dark steps, without any idea where I was going.

I'd find out soon enough.

# 24

As I continued down the steps, I was enveloped in darkness—but the strange, crystal pyramid I was holding began to glow! It began to emit a strange, green light that soon glowed so brightly that it lit up the entire cave!

Shadows shrunk away as I continued down the stone stairs. Soon, the steps stopped, and I was standing inside the tomb.

*What now?* I thought. *What am I supposed to do now?* But suddenly, a secret door slid open! A rock wall slid away, exposing a dark cave, beckoning me to enter.

Slowly, ever so slowly, I walked across the

tomb and into the cave. The pyramid lit up the walls and I stood for a moment, looking at my surroundings. Dark, black openings swelled from the walls of the caves.

Tunnels.

*Great,* I thought. *How am I supposed to know which way to go?*

Strangely enough, right when I had that thought, the pyramid began to dim, then it grew brighter. It was like the pyramid was answering my thoughts! I held it out before me, and it went dim. I found that when I moved the pyramid back and forth, it grew brighter and dimmer.

But there was more. There was a pattern to the changing brightness of the object. As I raised the pyramid in front of each cave, the pyramid grew brighter!

And when I raised the object to one cave in particular, it glowed like the sun!

*Was it telling me something? Was this what Rhaman meant when he said that the pyramid would guide me?*

I decided that I couldn't waste any more time trying to figure it out. I would have to trust the glowing pyramid.

I walked toward the tunnel. As if it were responding, the pyramid glowed even brighter. I was sure that I was doing the right thing.

Just before I stepped into the tunnel, I had the strange feeling of being watched.

I stopped.

I could *feel* it.

There was something watching me. I knew it.

I turned slowly to my left.

Nothing.

I turned slowly to my right.

*Eyes.* I could see two enormous eyes glaring at me from the inky black of one of the tunnels.

And I knew what they were. Oh, yes, I'd seen eyes like these a hundred times.

They were the eyes of a snake. Terrible, wicked eyes. They reflected the glowing pyramid in my hand.

Then I could hear movement. The eyes drew nearer, and I began to make out the snake's features.

"You're not real," I said aloud, remembering the words of Rhaman. However, I was still unsure myself.

Was it real? Or was it like the other strange things I had witnessed in the past day?

Suddenly, the huge snake opened his mouth.

My eyes bulged in horror. I gasped. My mind whirred furiously.

I had expected to see two fangs, or a row of teeth, or a tongue, or something. You know . . . like a normal snake.

But this snake was anything but normal. What came out of the snake's mouth was terrifying.

# 25

Snakes. Hundreds of them. When the giant snake opened his mouth, hundreds of smaller, baby snakes came out. It was the grossest thing I've ever seen in my life.

The smaller snakes hissed and swayed, back and forth, ready to strike. I was scared out of my mind.

I backed away, holding the crystal pyramid before me.

*"Remember, Josh . . . it's not real. Much of what you will see is not real."*

It was Rhaman's voice! It was coming from the pyramid!

"You're not real," I said out loud to the hundreds of hissing snakes. "You're not real. You're not real."

In the next instant, the enormous snake closed his mouth. All of the tiny snakes were gone — but what happened next was unbelievable.

The snake shrunk and changed. In seconds, I was no longer looking at a snake, but just an ordinary stick that was no longer than my arm!

"Can . . . can I talk to you?" I said out loud, peering into the pyramid.

No answer. The pyramid continued to glow, but apparently Rhaman couldn't hear me.

*Now what?* I thought. There were four different tunnels leading in four different directions. Which way should I go?

Suddenly, the pyramid moved in my hands all by itself! It seemed to be pulling me in the direction of one of the tunnels!

*Okay*, I thought. *Here goes nothing.*

I stepped into the dark tunnel and began to walk.

And walk.

And walk more.

Farther. Deeper. The tunnel grew wider, then smaller. Wider again. It felt like I had walked a thousand miles.

Then, the tunnel abruptly stopped. It just stopped at a solid rock wall.

"Okay," I said aloud, holding the glowing pyramid before me. "It must be another one of those trick doors. Open sesame."

Nothing. No door opened, and nothing happened.

Had I taken a wrong turn? The thought of having to go all the way back terrified me. Robyn was in trouble, and if I didn't get to her quick, she'd be made into a mummy!

*What do I do?* I thought. I looked around. The glowing pyramid in my hand provided plenty of light.

And it was then that I noticed the symbol on the rock wall in front of me.

The Eye. The Eye of Horus.

It was very faint, but when I drew closer, I could see it.

I reached out and touched it with my hand. I certainly didn't know it at the time, but I was about to discover a passageway into one of the most bizarre worlds I'd ever imagined.

# 26

The moment my hand touched the wall, the wall seemed to turn to glass. It shimmered and wavered, and suddenly it became transparent. I could actually see right *through* the stone!

And what I saw was amazing.

I was standing at the edge of a desert. The sky was blue and sand stretched on for miles.

But the most incredible thing of all was an enormous pyramid. It must have been a mile wide at its base, and the stone structure seemed to touch the sky.

As I looked on in amazement, I saw other things, too.

Mummies.

They were walking all around the giant pyramid like zombies. Strange beasts were everywhere. I saw an odd creature that looked like a cross between a dog and a horse. Another creature looked like a possum with wings.

I wished I would have brought my camera! No one on earth was going to believe what I was seeing.

But then I remembered: what I was seeing probably wasn't real, like Rhaman had said. I was sure that they would disappear just like the snake.

The crystal pyramid in my hand suddenly began to glow. I gazed into the hazy glass and saw shapes and forms develop. They were fuzzy at first, then became clear.

It was *me!* The crystal object in my hand showed me walking across the desert to the giant stone pyramid! Is that where I was supposed to go?

"To the pyramid?" I asked aloud, gazing into the crystal.

The pyramid in my hand suddenly glowed like

the sun.

"I guess that's a 'yes'," I said, and stepped into the bright sunlight. I started walking toward the giant stone pyramid.

I could still see the strange, zombie-like mummies walking all around. And the weird creatures, too. They were everywhere.

But as I got closer, they didn't even seem to notice me. It was as if I wasn't even there. As I walked closer and closer to the pyramid, I couldn't help but stare at the weird things that were all around. They were wandering aimlessly, as if they had nothing else to do. Getting to the giant pyramid was going to be a piece of cake.

I thought.

There was a big square-shaped hole at the base of the pyramid, and I figured that it was probably some sort of entryway into the large structure. I headed for it, all the while watching the odd creatures walking all around me.

Suddenly, one mummy spotted me. He stopped in his tracks, raised one arm, and began to moan. Soon, other mummies had stopped and turned. They began walking toward me, arms outstretched. Their moaning filled the air.

*Now what?* I wondered. *I've got a whole army of mummies after me!*

I ran to the pyramid. The soft sand pulled at my tennis shoes, and it was hard going. If you've ever tried to run in beach sand, you know what I'm talking about. Thankfully, the mummies didn't move very fast, and it was easy to stay ahead of them.

When I reached the base of the enormous pyramid I stopped. The thing was gargantuan! It looked like it went up into the sky forever.

But hundreds of mummies were coming my way! It was like an entire army of them!

I ran to the large doorway and ducked inside. I figured that I would have to rely on the crystal pyramid to give me directions.

But when I dashed through the doorway, I realized my mistake too late . . . *because the passage led nowhere!* There were no doors or other tunnels.

I stopped and turned around — and gasped in horror.

Mummies. Hundreds of them. They had

reached the entrance to the pyramid, blocking my escape. The mummies were looking at me, their arms reaching out, like they were going to grab me. Some of them were moaning.

*They aren't real,* I thought. *They aren't real. They're just like the snake that I saw.*

I closed my eyes and squeezed them shut. I opened them.

The mummies were still here . . . only now, they were coming toward me!

I was trapped! There was no way out!

# 27

The hoard of mummies slowly came closer, moaning and groaning, arms outstretched, reaching for me. I could hear their hot breath as they came closer and closer.

I frantically searched for a secret door. Could there be one? Was there some kind of hidden panel that would open up?

No. There was nothing. Only solid rock.

The mummies came. One of them reached for me and I tried to back up, but there was nowhere to go.

The mummy grasped my shoulder. I screamed, but I knew that no one would be able to hear my cries.

The mummy that had grabbed my shoulder suddenly stopped. He was looking right at me, and I stared into his eyes and saw . . . *fear?* Was he afraid of me? The mummy suddenly looked like he'd seen a ghost.

He released his grip on my shoulder and backed away, groaning and pointing at me.

"*Eeeeyyyyyyyyeeeee,*" the mummy groaned. Soon, all of the mummies were groaning, saying the same thing.

The eye! They were afraid of the eye that Rhaman had painted on my forehead!

I grew bolder, and took a step toward the retreating mummies.

"Go on!" I said, shaking my fist at them. "Go! And don't come back!"

The swarm of mummies continued to back away, out of the pyramid and into the sun.

Whew. That had been another close one.

But now what would I do? I had to save Robyn, and fast. But Rhaman hadn't had time to explain what to do. He just said that the Stone of Titan would help me.

"Well, what now?" I said aloud to the stone. I was standing at the foot of the pyramid, and most of the mummies had gone back to their business of simply walking around and moaning.

Suddenly, a strange mist began to form inside the crystal pyramid in my hand! It grew thick like smoke and it swirled and whirled about in the glossy stone, then it began to clear. Objects began to form.

"Holy smokes!" I exclaimed when I saw what was in the crystal pyramid.

It was me! In the Stone of Titan, I could see myself standing at the very top of a huge pyramid, about to enter a door.

Is that what I was supposed to do? Was I supposed to climb to the top of the pyramid?

I looked up, staring at the awesome stone structure that towered over me. There were no steps, nothing I could grab onto and pull myself up.

I stared into the Stone of Titan and watched myself at the top of the pyramid. It was freaky, like I was looking into the future or something.

All of a sudden, a loud screech from behind me

caused me to jump. I spun.

A giant winged creature was almost upon me! It flew like a bird, but it had the face of a cat! Fur was all over its body, except on its wings which were covered with black feathers. It was big, too. The size of a horse!

And I knew right then that I wouldn't be making it to the top of the pyramid — because in the next instant, the strange cat-bird reached out with two long claws and grasped both of my shoulders.

I had been captured!

I knew I was a goner.

The creature grabbed my shoulders with so much force that I almost dropped the Stone of Titan! Two seconds later I was dragged up into the air, kicking and screaming.

"Hey, you nasty flying cat!" I shouted. "Put me down! Put me down!"

Do you think it listened to me? No way. No matter how much I struggled, the weird creature kept flying higher and higher.

But wait a minute! As we flew higher, we were getting closer to the top of the pyramid! Was the creature taking me to the top of the pyramid?

*Yes!* That's exactly what he was doing! He was taking me to the top of the enormous stone structure!

I clung tightly to the stone in my hand as we flew up, higher and higher. When we reached the top of the pyramid, the creature slowed. There was a ledge right at the very top, and I could see the dark entrance of a doorway that led inside.

The creature hovered right above the ledge, its wings beating the air. Ever so gently, it lowered me to the ledge. When my feet touched the ground it loosed its grip and let me go. The creature wasted no time in flying off.

"Thanks for the lift!" I called out after the beast.

I looked around. From where I was, high in the sky, I could see for miles and miles and miles. There were other pyramids in the distance! They looked like mountains in the desert. The blue sky was endless. I had no idea where I was, but I don't think we have any place like this on earth! Certainly not a place with mummies walking all around and weird creatures running everywhere!

I turned around and looked into the doorway. It was rectangular, just like you'd expect. There was no door, just an opening.

And steps. Stone steps went down into the pyramid. I peered down, and the steps disappeared into darkness.

I must admit, I was afraid. So many bizarre things had happened. Yet, as I looked down into the darkness of the pyramid, I knew that I was going to have to be careful. I was entering Akbar's territory now, and anything could happen. I really did not want to go down those steps.

But I would. Somewhere, inside this giant pyramid, Robyn was in trouble. She needed my help.

I held the Stone of Titan as tightly as I could. "I hope you help me out a little bit," I whispered to the crystal.

I took one step through the door and down the first stair. Then another. My sneakers were silent upon the chiseled stone.

The sunlight faded, and I was now in the shade of the entryway.

"Here goes nothing," I whispered, taking another step, then another. I looked back at the blue sky, wondering if it was the last time I would see it. Then I turned back.

Slowly, cautiously, I proceeded into the depths of the pyramid . . . into the lair of Akbar the Terrible.

# 29

The steps seemed to go on forever.

Down I went into the pyramid, farther and farther, deeper and deeper. The farther I went, the darker it became.

But I got a surprise.

The Stone of Titan began to glow! It glowed a bright, powdery-blue, and it lit up the passageway like daylight! I still didn't know exactly where I was going, but at least I could see.

I continued down the winding stairs in the glow of the mysterious crystal pyramid. Now that I could see, my progress was much faster. I knew that time was short and I'd have to move fast.

After traveling for what seemed like hours, the steps suddenly stopped. I found myself in a large room. The ceiling was very high, and were it not for the glow of the crystal in my hand, I would be in complete darkness.

The walls were covered completely with hieroglyphics. From the floor to the ceiling, strange writing filled every wall.

But it was a drawing on the far wall that caught my attention.

The eye. It was the same, strange eye that I'd seen in the sky. The same eye that we'd spotted in the tomb. The very eye that Rhaman had painted on my forehead.

The Eye of Horus.

I walked across the room, my eyes focused on the eye on the wall. It was bigger than most of the drawings.

I stopped a few feet away and held out the glowing crystal in my hand. The eye seemed to be staring back at me, looking at me. As I looked on, I noticed something peculiar.

Right in the very center of the eye, there was a

hand print in the stone. It was hardly noticeable. It wasn't colored, and it blended right in with the rest of the rock. But there was no mistake. It was a hand print — a human hand print — like someone had placed their hand in wet cement.

Holding on to the Stone of Titan with one hand, I reached up and placed my free hand to the hand print. The stone was cold and damp.

But the strangest thing happened.

The wall began to disappear!

As I held my hand to the rock, the entire wall began to fade. It grew real gray and watery, and then it became transparent.

But it was what was on the other side of the wall that caused me alarm.

*Lava.* I could see a bed of molten lava, bubbling and boiling. The coals were red and orange and yellow, and I could see hot steam rising from the lake of melted rock.

Suddenly, the pyramid that was in my hand flew up into the air! It floated for a moment, then slipped through the invisible wall. My hand was still in the air, pressed into the hand print, except that the wall was gone. I could actually feel cold stone beneath my hand, but the wall had vanished. When I pushed my hand, it moved just like there was nothing there.

I took a step through the wall, and reached out to grasp the crystal pyramid suspended in the air. As I tried to grab it, it moved farther away. I took another step toward it. By now, it was obvious that I was to follow it.

The glowing crystal led me to the lava bed. Below me, the orange and red goop churned and boiled. Then, the Stone of Titan floated along the edge of the lava. I followed it around a narrow ledge at the edge of the cave. There was only a thin path to walk on, and if I wasn't careful, I'd plummet into the bed of lava below. It was a good thing that I didn't have to hang on to the crystal, because I used both hands to hang on to the rock wall as I walked.

The ledge finally opened up at the far edge of the lava bed. The crystal lowered, and I reached my hand out and grabbed it.

Where to now? There were five cave-like doors that pretty much looked the same. Which one should I go through? Should I go through any at all?

A sudden, sharp scream made up my mind for me.  It was a scream of terror and fright.

And I knew who it was.

*Robyn.*

# PART FIVE:

# AKBAR'S

# LAIR

# 30

I sprang so quickly that I almost dropped the crystal pyramid. Robyn's cry came from the tunnel entrance on my far right, and I ran to it.

It opened into a big, cavernous room. There were urns and vases of gold and silver everywhere! Mummies were moving about like sloths, and I could hear them murmuring to themselves.

And on the far side of the cave —

*Robyn!*

And man, was she in trouble. Mummies were wrapping her up in linen! They were going to make a mummy out of her!

And sitting on a golden throne, watching everything, was Akbar the Terrible. He wore a colored turban on his head, and a coat of dazzling gold and silver, like many of the items that filled the cave. Both of his hands rested on the arms of the chairs, and he seemed to be enjoying himself.

"Careful," he called out to the mummies. "She'll be wearing her new suit for a long, long time. I want it to be perfect!"

Robyn screamed again, and I could see her struggle to get away from the mummies. They were just finishing wrapping her up, and were about to put her into a large stone coffin.

I had to do something . . . *fast.*

"Hey!" I shouted. "Knock it off right now!"

The mummies stopped moving. Akbar the Terrible snapped his head around. Robyn froze, peering through the white cloth wrapped around her head.

Silence. There was dead silence for nearly two whole seconds. You could have heard a pin drop.

Suddenly, Akbar the Terrible raised his arm and pointed an accusing finger at me.

"Mummies! Seize him!" he boomed. "Seize

him! Quickly!"

The mummies began to walk toward me. I was still standing in the opening of the cavern, and I looked for somewhere to run.

But there was nowhere to go! The only place I could run to is back the way I came . . . or into another cave. I remembered the snake that I'd come across earlier, and decided that I'd have to take my chances with the mummies.

They kept coming. They were moving slow, but they were coming. In a few moments, they would be upon me.

At the far side of the cave, Robyn was struggling frantically to get out of the tightly-wound linen. She was having a tough time, but she was managing.

As for me, I wasn't sure what I was going to do. I knew that the mummies outside the pyramid were afraid of the eye on my forehead, and I hoped that maybe these mummies were, too.

"Hurry!" Akbar shouted. "Do not let him escape!"

Without warning, the crystal pyramid in my

hand began floating in the air! It raised up just above my head and hung, glowing brightly.

The mummies stopped walking. They stopped their nonsensical murmuring. One by one, they began to back away.

"What are you doing?!?!" shouted Akbar. "What are you—" when he saw the glowing pyramid suspended in the air, he stopped in mid-sentence. His hands fell, and he stood up. His baggy purple pants billowed out around him, and he placed his hands on his waist.

"So," he began, glaring at me. "You've been talking to my brother. Ha! A lot of good that will do you. Now that I have this—" he reached into his pocket and pulled out the ankh. "Now that I have this, I am much more powerful than my brother."

With a single wave of his hand the crystal pyramid was sent spinning! It was knocked out of the air by some unseen force. It tumbled behind me and landed right near the edge of the lava pit.

I knew that, no matter what, I had to have the pyramid. Without it, how would we ever find a way out?

That is, of course, if we ever got the chance to get out. Right now, it wasn't looking very good.

I spun on my heels and ran to the pyramid, scooping it up with one sweeping motion.

Suddenly, I stopped.

There was a face in the pyramid! It was the face of Rhaman! And he was speaking to me!

"Josh!" he said. "Listen carefully. There is only one thing that Akbar needs to become supreme ruler. The shen. I know where it is. Now it is time for you to know, too. Listen carefully, and I will guide you to it."

But when Rhaman told me what I was going to have to do, I simply couldn't believe it.

*Rhaman told me that I was going to have to dive into the lava!*

That's right! That's exactly what he said! He said that the shen was at the bottom of the pool of lava.

But what he said next was even more unbelievable.

"The lava is not really lava," Rhaman explained. "It is only water."

"Water?" I replied. "But how?"

"A long time ago when I hid the shen, I knew that anyone could dive into a pool of water to find it. But no one would dive into a pool of lava. So, using the magic of the ages, I created an illusion. What you see only *looks* like lava. It's actually *water*. Even Akbar thinks that it is lava."

I glanced over the edge of the cliff and looked down. It sure looked like lava to me!

"You must hurry," Rhaman said. "There is not much time left. It will be bad enough if Akbar can steal this pyramid from you. Then, nothing will stop him. He will use the Stone of Titan to find the shen, and then he will become the Supreme Ruler."

*Are you out of your mind?* I thought.

"No," he replied.

*He heard me! He heard my thoughts!*

"But . . . but I can feel the heat of the lava," I said.

"I know what it feels like," Rhaman replied. "But it is not as it seems. Please—you must hurry, before it is too late. Your friend needs your help. I need your help."

Without warning, Akbar's voice boomed through the air.

"Ha! There you are! Now I will take what is mine!"

In the crystal pyramid, Rhaman's face looked back at me.

"You must go," he insisted. "You won't be harmed. I promise you. Go. Now!"

I couldn't believe what he was asking me to do. But I had to trust him. I had to do what he asked.

And when Akbar the Terrible took a step in my direction, there was only one thing I could do.

I took a deep breath, tucked the crystal pyramid under my arm, and leapt into the pool of lava.

# 32

I knew that it was over. As I fell toward the steaming pool of molten rock, I knew that I had lost my mind. I was plummeting faster and faster toward the red-hot bed of coals. In seconds, my goose would be cooked.

And suddenly, it happened. I hit the surface of the coals.

But instead of getting fried like I thought I would, it was just like Rhaman said: I found myself in nothing but water! The water was warm, and it was very comfortable.

I opened my eyes and received still another shock: *I was swimming in an underwater city!*

Below me, I saw buildings and stone structures made of white stone.

And creatures! There were strange sea creatures swimming all about. Some of them looked like seahorses, and some looked like huge shrimp. They swam past me and all around me, and they seemed to be smiling.

I kept swimming down until I had reached the bottom. It was really strange, seeing this underwater city that surrounded me.

Just then, I heard Rhaman's voice. It sounded distant and far away.

"You will find the shen on a table in the building directly in front of you. Go ahead, go and get it. You will not be harmed by any of these creatures. They are the guardians of the shen, and they have been expecting you."

I tried to walk, but it is pretty hard underwater. I found I could just move better by swimming.

And another odd thing: I didn't feel the need to breathe! I can hold my breath for about thirty seconds before the tightness in my lungs told me that I needed to exhale and get more air. Yet, for some strange reason, I felt fine.

The building that Rhaman told me to enter was quite big. It was pure white with a large entryway. As I approached, sea creatures of all shapes and sizes whirled about, as if leading me on. They seemed quite happy that I was there.

I swam through the entryway, and on a table in the middle of the room . . . .

*The shen.*

It looked just like Rhaman had described . . . a gold circle with a single, horizontal bar under it. It was larger than the ankh that I had found, and it shined like a new moon, giving off a strange light in this underwater world.

I wasted no time in swimming to the table and picking up the shen. It was too big to put into my pocket, so I carried it in the same hand that held the Stone of Titan.

I swam out of the building and into the city. All around me, sea creatures tumbled and flipped about in the water. They were kind of cool, and I wondered what it would be like to have one as a pet.

I kicked my feet, slowly rising to the surface. The strange sea creatures continued to swim about, as if they were my protectors. When I neared the surface, they backed away.

I was alone.

What was going to happen? I was almost at the surface, and I knew that Akbar the terrible would be waiting for me, along with his wrapped-up army of mummies.

My head broke the surface, and I received a shock. Although I knew I was swimming in water, all around me was *lava!* I should be getting roasted right now, but I wasn't even warm!

But the real shock came when I looked up and saw Akbar the Terrible.

One arm was raised and he was clenching his fist . . . and in the other arm—

*A spear.* It had a large, sharp tip. Without warning, Akbar drew his arm back, aimed right for me . . . and threw the spear.

# 33

The spear sailed through the air, heading right for me. There was no way I could escape its path.

Just then, the shen that I had been holding in my hand sprang from the water! At first I thought that I had dropped it, but when it popped out of the water, I couldn't believe my eyes! It spun in the air directly in front of me . . . and the spear hit it! Sparks flew and metal clanged. The spear fell into the lava-water and disappeared. The shen hung in the air.

I looked up at Akbar, and he had a look of amazement on his face.

"The shen!" he cried loudly. "You've found the

mystical shen!  Give it to me!"

Right.  Like I'm going to hand it over to him just because he wants it.

"No way," I said.  The shen lowered to the lava, and I reached out and grasped it.

"Please," he begged.  "It is very powerful. You don't know how to use its special magic, but I can show you.  I can show you, and together, you and I will be rulers of the kingdom!"

I shook my head, and began to swim as best as I could to the opposite side of the lava pool.

"You have no idea what you're doing!" Akbar the Terrible shouted at me.  "You can't use the shen!  You don't know enough about it!"

I reached the other side of the pool of lava. Here, it was easier to climb out.  I struggled to my feet.

*"Josh!  Look out!"*

I knew that voice!  That was the voice of Robyn!

I spun.  Robyn was now standing near one of the entryways to the caves.  She'd succeeded in pulling most of the linen wrappings from her body.

And she'd warned me just in time. Now Akbar was charging madly, running on the ledge alongside the pool of lava. He had a large gold sword in his hand.

"Well then," he boomed, as he sprinted closer and closer. "Then I'll just have to *take* the shen from you!"

And suddenly he was towering above me, sword held high.

Carrying the shen and the crystal pyramid, I dashed back, but there was nowhere to go. The only thing behind me was a solid wall of rock.

Akbar the Terrible raised his awful sword, and came at me. I prepared myself for the worst.

# 34

And then I heard the voice.

At the very last moment, I heard a voice.

Rhaman.

*"Do not worry, my friend."* It was all he said.

*Right,* I thought. *He's not the one with a madman attacking him.*

All of a sudden I knew what he meant. The shen! The shen was the symbol of eternity! Whoever had the shen could never be harmed! It would protect me!

I held out the object in my hand just as Akbar brought his sword down.

What happened next was incredible. The shen

took on a life of its own, snapping up into the air. With the force of a train and the fury of a lion it lashed out and struck Akbar in the stomach. The impact sent him flying backwards, out of balance. He dropped the sword.

But the shen wasn't done with its work just yet. It kept pushing Akbar, pushing him back, farther and farther, closer and closer to the pool of lava-water. Akbar kept trying to grab the shen that was pushing him harder and harder. Suddenly, Akbar went over the ledge—and fell into the bubbling, churning pool.

Upon finding himself in harmless water, and not the boiling hot lava that he expected, Akbar began to swim.

He didn't get far, because—

*The sea creatures!* The sea creatures suddenly swarmed about him just below the surface. I could see them beneath the churning, swirling lava-water.

*"Aaahhhhh!"* Akbar screamed. "Stop them! *Stop them!"* He tried to fight off the creatures, but it was no use. When I had been beneath the surface, they had seemed friendly.

At least, they were friendly to *me*.

Without any warning, Akbar disappeared beneath the surface. In seconds, the only thing that remained of Akbar the Terrible was his golden sword that lay near the pool of lava.

Robyn was pulling off the last few pieces of linen from her clothing. All of the mummies were gone. We were alone in the cave.

I ran to her side. "Man, I'm glad I found you in time," I said.

"Me too," she breathed. "Me too."

"Are you alright?"

"Yes. For a while, though, I thought I was going to be wrapped in that gooey stuff forever."

I looked around. "Well, let's get out of here," I said. "The Stone of Titan lead me to you. It will help lead us back to Mackinaw City."

"The Stone of what?" Robyn asked. "That glass thing you were carrying in your hand?"

"Yeah. It's—"

I stopped speaking, because I suddenly realized that I no longer had the stone! I spun around, looking for it, but it was nowhere to be found!

"It's gone!" I exclaimed. "I was carrying it . . . and now it's gone!"

Robyn pointed. "I saw it fall and break when that thing flew out of your hands and hit that mean dude," she said.

"Oh no!" I said. "That was the Stone of Titan! Rhaman gave that to me so it could lead me to you, and lead us out of here!

We walked to where I had dropped the crystal pyramid. Sure enough, there were shards of crystal all over the ground.

The Stone of Titan was shattered. The stone was broken, and we were lost . . . somewhere, in another time, another world.

And then, an amazing thing happened . . . .

# 35

We heard a gurgling noise in the pool of lava-water, and we turned.

Something was emerging.

"Get back!" I shouted. "It might be Akbar!"

We ran to the entrance of one of the caves. I didn't know where we would go if Akbar returned, but as it turned out, we wouldn't have to worry — because what came out of the lava was the shen . . . followed by the ankh! They floated in the air above the pool, then they began to whirl around. Then, both objects drifted over to the entrance of a cave on the opposite side of the pool. They hung there in the air, as if they were dangling by strings.

"What in the world?" Robyn breathed.

"They're showing us the way out!" I cried. "Come on! they'll lead us back to the tomb! Back to Mackinaw City!"

"I hope you're right," Robyn replied.

We rushed carefully around the pool of lava. Sure enough, as we approached the floating objects, they began to drift into the cave.

"See?" I said. "We're supposed to follow them. They will lead us home. I know they will."

And so, we followed the two floating objects. It sure was weird, knowing that the ankh and the shen weren't supported by anything. They drifted about like they were lighter than air.

We walked for hours. Or, at least, that's what it seemed like. Up and down, around corners,. Through dark tunnels and caverns.

Just when I began to think that we would never make it home, I saw something shimmer up ahead.

*The tomb!*

"We made it!" I shouted. I began running down the tunnel, and so did Robyn. The ankh and the shen were hovering in the tomb above a silver vase. Rhaman was there, and when Robyn saw him, she gasped.

"Run!" she shouted.

"No," I said, grabbing her arm. "That's Rhaman. He's the one who helped me find you!"

Rhaman bowed. "Pleased to meet you," he said. He turned to me. "You have done well, my young friend. Very well indeed."

The ankh and the shen were still hanging weightless in the air. Rhaman reached out and snapped them up. Instantly, the two objects regained their weight and sat heavily in the palm of Rhaman's hand.

"What is going to happen now?" I asked.

"Nothing," Rhaman replied. "That is what is so wonderful. Akbar the Terrible has been stopped. We are all safe."

"But what about this place?" I asked. "What about the tomb?"

"Come," Rhaman replied, motioning with his hands. He walked up the steps and we followed him into the bright sunshine.

Ah, daylight. It had been a long time.

"I must ask you both to keep this secret," Rhaman began. "This tomb is not meant to be disturbed. You must tell no one what you've seen here today."

Robyn and I nodded our heads in agreement. We wouldn't tell a soul. Besides . . . who would believe us?

"Here." Rhaman held out his hand, offering the ankh. "Go on. Take it. It is a gift. Now that Akbar is gone forever, I will not need it."

I took the ankh and looked at it, rolling it over in my hand.

"You can use the ankh whenever you need to find your way. If you ever become lost and need to find your way safely, the ankh will guide you."

"Cool!" I said, turning the object over in my hand. "Thank you!"

"And now I must go," Rhaman said. "It is too dangerous to be in your world. Farewell, my friends."

"But . . . but what about the tomb?" I stammered. "It's all dug up. If someone comes along, they'll find it."

"Watch," he said. With that, Rhaman turned

and walked down the steps into the tomb.

After a few seconds, strange things began to happen. We could feel the ground tremble beneath our feet. Suddenly, the door of the tomb closed—all by itself! Dirt began swirling in little tornadoes, and holes began to fill themselves in. It was freaky! Robyn and I watched in silence as things about us moved on their own.

In less than a minute, the tomb had been re-buried. The ground was solid, and it didn't look at all like anyone had been digging there.

"I think I've had enough weird excitement for one day," Robyn said.

"Yeah, me too," I replied. "Let's go home."

$$\bullet \ \bullet \ \bullet$$

That night, I met Robyn downtown. There were lots of people walking around and shopping in stores. We each bought ice cream, and then we walked down to the park. Neither one of us spoke about the events that had happened earlier in the day.

"Well, it's getting late," Robyn said, looking up

at the star-filled sky. Though it was almost nine o'clock, there were still a lot of people wandering about downtown.

"Yeah," I said. "I've got to get home, too. See you tomorrow."

I watched Robyn walk away, and I thought about the strange things that had happened earlier that day. I wished that I could tell someone, but I made a promise to Rhaman. I would have to keep everything a secret.

But I still had the ankh.

I dug my hand into my pocket and pulled out the object. I was glad that Rhaman gave it to me.

"What's that?" a voice behind me asked.

I turned to find a kid about my age. He was eating a slab of fudge with one hand, and pointing to my ankh with the other.

"Oh, it's just a souvenir," I replied. "I picked it up here in Mackinaw City."

"It looks cool," he said.

I handed it to him and he examined it for a moment, then handed it back to me.

"My name is Rick," he said. "Rick Owens."

"Hi, Rick. I'm Josh."

We talked for a few minutes, and he said that he was here with his family on vacation.

"How do you like it so far?" I asked.

"Oh, it's great," he replied, popping the last bit of fudge into his mouth. "It's safe here."

I didn't know what he meant by that.

"What do you mean 'safe'?" I asked.

"There are no weird creatures or monsters here," he replied, looking around.

If only I could have told him about what had happened to Robyn and I earlier that day!

But I still didn't know what he meant.

"Monsters?" I asked. "Creatures?"

He nodded his head. "Yep. I just got back from summer camp. There was a small lake there filled with Mega-Monsters."

"Filled with what?!?!" I asked, my eyes wide. "What's a Mega-Monster?!?!?!"

And what he told me was far scarier than the adventure Robyn and I had been through. In fact, what Rick Owens told me was scarier than anything I'd ever heard in my life . . . .

Introducing a
**BRAND NEW SERIES**
from Johnathan Rand:

*Turn the page to read the first few chapters of*
*#1 in the* ***'American Chillers'*** *series:*

# The Michigan
# Mega-Monsters

# 1

Summer camp is supposed to be fun. It's supposed to be games and swimming and hot dogs and campfires and silly pranks.

It's *supposed* to be.

But not this year. Not at Camp Willow. What I went through at Camp Willow was one of the most horrifying experiences of my life.

To get to the camp, I rode the bus with a bunch of other kids. It was a long ride. I live in Grand Rapids, and Camp Willow is near Rochester Hills, which is on the other side of the state.

My name was being called just as I was getting off the bus. There was a man with a megaphone, holding it to his mouth and speaking. He was standing with a group of a dozen kids that were about my age. Other buses had arrived, and their passengers were unloading.

"Last call for Rick Owens!" his voice boomed out. "Is there a Rick Owens here?"

"Right here!" I hollered out, slinging my heavy pack over my shoulder.

"Hurry it up! We haven't got all day!"

*Jeepers*, I thought. *I just got here. Give me a break.*

I joined the group of waiting campers. They were all my age, boys and girls. I didn't recognize any of them.

"Campers! Welcome to Camp Willow!" the man with the megaphone blurted out. "My name is Mr. Leonard, and I'll be your patrol leader. Take a few minutes to make sure you have all of your gear, and then we'll assign you to your cabins."

Camp Willow is really cool. There is a main lodge and about ten cabins that surround Willow Lake, which is pretty small. In fact, you won't find the camp or the lake on any map. But kids from all over Michigan—even from around the country—come here every year. It's a popular camp, and I'd been waiting all summer.

Of course, that was before everything happened.

Before the Mega-Monsters.

Oh, you can think what you want. But Mega-Monsters exist.

I know. I saw them. So did my friends. And the terror would begin that very first night at camp.

# 2

My group was called the Wolf Patrol. I was assigned a cabin with five other guys, and we stored our gear and then met for a short patrol meeting around the big fire pit. Mr. Leonard handed out a sheet of rules, and then we all took a few minutes to meet one another in the group.

"I'm Rick Owens," I said to a girl standing to the left of me. "I'm from Grand Rapids."

"I'm Leah," she said. "Leah Warner. I'm from Saginaw." She had a friendly smile, and she was a little taller than I.

A blonde-haired girl in front of us turned around. "I've been to Saginaw," she said, her eyes lighting up. "My family travels through

Saginaw when we go north to visit Mackinac Island. My name is Sandy Johnson."

We talked for a few minutes. I liked Leah and Sandy. They were pretty cool. I met some other kids in our patrol that were from other states. One kid came all the way from California!

The rest of the day was spent getting to know our way around the camp. Our patrol leader took us around and showed us different things like where the camp store was, where to go in case of an emergency, and where the mess hall was. The mess hall was a huge room in the main lodge where all of the campers gathered three times a day for meals. Our first meal in the mess hall was going to be at seven o'clock the next morning.

After we were shown around Camp Willow, the rest of the evening was free time. I wandered down by the lake and talked with Leah and Sandy. We were all excited about the things we would be doing during the week. Fishing, hiking, swimming, canoeing . . . this was going to be the best week of the summer!

I had a hard time falling asleep that night. I was so excited. Finally, after counting a billion sheep, I finally fell asleep.

But not for long.

I was awakened by a terrible nightmare. It was *awful*. I dreamed that I was in my cabin and there were big, red eyes glowing in the window! The eyes belonged to a horrible creature, and in my dream I could hear him breathing just outside my window. He was looking at me the way a dog looks at a steak bone.

Suddenly, I awoke and sat straight up in bed. My heart was pounding, and I was breathing heavily. I'm not sure what time it was, but it was really dark. My bunkmates were all sleeping.

I turned to look out the window, afraid of what might be there.

Nothing.

*Whew*, I thought. *A dream. That's all it was.* I laid back down, and, after a while, I fell back asleep.

Next morning, I was jolted awake by a trumpeting bugle. It was *loud!* There was no way anyone was going to sleep through that!

I showered and dressed and got ready to go to the mess hall for breakfast—but when I walked out the door of the cabin, I got the shock of my life.

There, in the soft earth, were footprints. Not human footprints, but strange, claw-like footprints, much bigger than a human's.

*And the footprints led right up to the window by my bed!*

# 3

At the mess hall, I sat with Sandy and Leah. I told them about my dream and about the tracks beneath my window.

"That's pretty freaky," Leah said.

"In your dream, did you see what the creature looked like?" Sandy asked.

"Not really," I said. "It had red eyes, and maybe a big nose. I guess I don't remember anything else, except the fact that it was gross-looking."

"It was probably just someone trying to scare you, that's all," Leah offered. She took a sip of orange juice and returned the glass to the table. "You know. Just a prank."

I shook my head. "Those footprints didn't look like they were made by a human," I said.

I sat quietly during the rest of breakfast. Sandy and Leah got along well, and they talked a lot to one another. All around me, dozens of kids talked and laughed and ate cereal and French toast. One dark-haired kid at the end of our table was really loud and obnoxious. He threw a strawberry and hit another kid on the other side of the mess hall, then pretended that he hadn't done anything. Every camp has a troublemaker, and it looked like he was going to be the one this week.

But I kept thinking about the creature in my dream. And the footprints.

*Leah is right*, I told myself. *It was probably someone just playing a prank. A joke. There is no such thing as monsters.*

Our patrol spent the morning hiking and learning the names of all the trees. I even caught a grass snake! Then we all went out in canoes and rowed around the lake. It was a blast! We splashed other kids in our patrol with our paddles, and by the time we were done, all of us were soaked. By lunchtime, I had forgotten all about my dream and the footprints.

Not for long.

Our afternoon activity was swimming. Our patrol, and several other patrols, met down by the beach. The day was hot and there wasn't a cloud in the sky.

Our patrol leader pointed to the buoys. "Nobody goes beyond that point," he ordered. "Stay in the swim area. Everybody understand?"

We all nodded and spoke up, eager to dive into the cool water.

"You've got thirty minutes. When the bell rings, get dried off and meet by the flagpole."

I was the first to hit the water, followed by my fellow members of the Wolf Patrol. The water was cool and fresh. There was a diving board at the end of the dock, and we took turns diving.

I guess Sandy hadn't been paying attention, because when I saw her, she was a few feet beyond the buoys . . . outside of the swim area.

"Sandy!" I called out. She turned her head. "You're outside of the swim area!"

She waved, and then began swimming back

toward shore.  I turned around to jump off the diving board . . . but in the next instant I was stopped by Sandy's piercing scream.  I spun, just in time to see a horrified look on her face.

"*SOMETHING'S GOT ME!*" she screamed in panic. "*IT'S GOT ME!  IT'S GOT MY LEG!*"

Suddenly, she was pulled beneath the surface. Sandy was gone.

# 4

I ran down the end of the dock and plunged into the water. A lifeguard was at his post and he, too, dove into the water to help.

All of a sudden, Sandy's head popped above the surface. She was sputtering and coughing.

"Hang on Sandy!" I shouted as I crawled arm over arm through the water.

Just then, another head emerged right next to Sandy. It was the dark-haired kid that threw the strawberry during breakfast.

"Ha ha ha!" he smirked. "Gotcha!"

"Jerk!" Sandy scolded.

"Fooled ya, fooled ya," the kid teased, swimming away.

I reached Sandy. "What happened?" I asked.

"That kid snuck up under me and grabbed my ankle and pulled me under," she said sharply. By now, Leah had swum up to us, and we all headed back to the dock. On shore, the lifeguard was scolding the dark-haired kid. He kicked him out of the water for the rest of the day.

"See?" Leah said smartly as she climbed up the wooden ladder to the dock. "He got what he deserved."

"I'll get him back somehow," Sandy said. She was really angry. "Maybe I'll sneak up to his cabin at night and scare the daylights out of him," she said.

I didn't think that she was serious — until later that night.

Sometime after midnight, I was awakened by screaming coming from the cabin next to mine. The kids had all of the lights on, and the dark-haired troublemaker was standing by the door with a flashlight, screaming something about a monster. That kid was really spooked!

I smiled. *You really got him back, Sandy*, I thought, climbing back into bed. *You got him good.*

The next morning, I found Leah and Sandy in the mess hall.

"Nice going!" I said to Sandy as I sat down.

She had a puzzled look on her face. "What do you mean?" she asked.

"Scaring that dark-haired goofball," I replied. "You know . . . last night."

"I didn't do anything," Sandy insisted, shaking her head. "I mean, I would have *liked* to, but I'm not going to do anything that is going to get me in trouble."

"You . . . you mean . . . that wasn't you last night? Scaring that kid?"

"Nope," Sandy assured me, shaking her head again. Her light blonde hair brushed her cheeks. "I was sound asleep."

Terror began to well up inside me. *If it wasn't Sandy playing a joke last night, then what did that kid see? Did he really see something?*

I had to know.

Without saying a word, I got up from the breakfast table and left the mess hall. I ran all the way to the kid's cabin, searching the ground.

It didn't take long.

On the ground, all around the cabin, were footprints—exactly like the ones I'd seen at my cabin yesterday morning!

# 5

The rumors about the monster began to spread. There were other kids that said they had spotted something, and lots of kids saw the tracks in the soft earth.

Was there really some strange creature stalking the campers? If so, where did it come from?

Our patrol was supposed to go fishing that day, but it started to rain. We gathered in the main lodge and played indoor games. Most of them were kind of boring, and I just kind of hung out and watched.

And thought about the monster that I had seen in my dream.

And the one that the dark-haired goofball had seen.

I decided that I would go and find the kid and talk to him. I knew he was a troublemaker, and I didn't like him . . . but I *had* to know. I *had* to know what he saw.

I couldn't find him in the main lodge, so I went to his cabin. The rain was starting to let up, and it looked like the sun might come out again.

I pounded on the door of the cabin.

"Hello?" I said. "Anybody here?"

No answer.

I pushed on the door, and it swung open.

"Anybody home?" I called out, stepping inside.

The cabin was tidy, but I noticed something odd.

Although there were six beds, only *five* beds had gear piled around. I thought all the cabins were supposed to be full.

I left the cabin and returned to the main lodge. Mr. Williams, the camp director, was in his office.

"Excuse me," I said, knocking on the open door as I spoke.

"Yes?" he said. He looked up from his pile of papers. "Everything okay?"

"Yes," I replied. "I was just looking for someone. I don't know his name, but he has dark hair and he—"

"He's gone," Mr. Williams said flatly. "Left an hour ago."

"Where did he go?" I asked.

"Home. Got scared. At least that's what I was told. His parents came and picked him up."

*Scared?* I thought. *He got so scared that he left camp?*

I found Leah and Sandy in the mess hall and told them about the kid leaving.

"Good," said Sandy. "Serves him right. At least we won't have to put up with him for the whole week."

But I wanted to know more. Whatever that kid saw, it scared him bad enough to leave.

And maybe I hadn't had a nightmare, after all. Maybe I really saw something.

That night, around the campfire, I was about to find out.

All of us in Wolf Patrol gathered around our

campfire. We roasted marshmallows and were telling jokes. The sun had gone down long ago, and a million stars dotted the sky. Everyone was having fun . . . until a chilling scream pierced the night.

Everyone around the campfire stopped talking. A chill raced down my spine. Not a word was spoken.

And then, we heard the crunching of branches, coming closer and closer.

"Who's there?" Mr. Leonard called out.

"Just me," said a very human, adult voice.

Whew! You could actually feel the relief in the air when we realized it was only one of the camp counselors.

His shadowy form came closer to the fire. When we saw him in the flickering light, our entire group gasped in horror.

From where I sat, it looked like the counselor was covered from head to toe — *in blood.*

*Look for*
**AMERICAN CHILLERS #1:**

*available now!*

# Mackinaw City Mummies Word Scramble!

yatepngi              _ _ _ _ _ _ _ _

btmo                      _ _ _ _

yummm                   _ _ _ _ _

ichrarntlewg          _ _ _ _ _ _ _ _ _ _

brkaa                     _ _ _ _ _

yrnbo                     _ _ _ _ _

kinmwaca iyct       _ _ _ _ _ _ _   _ _ _ _

lhvsoe                    _ _ _ _ _ _

kmommnane           _ _ _ _ _ _ _ _

anmhar                   _ _ _ _ _ _

ymadrip                 _ _ _ _ _ _ _

iantt                       _ _ _ _ _

knah                       _ _ _ _

yee fo srhuo       _ _ _  _ _  _ _ _ _ _

ganiicmh hrcilels  _ _ _ _ _ _ _ _  _ _ _ _ _ _ _

hanjnohat danr    _ _ _ _ _ _ _ _  _ _ _ _

imcenraa clreshli  _ _ _ _ _ _ _ _  _ _ _ _ _ _ _

shjo                       _ _ _ _

**Connect the characters with the book they belong in:**

| | |
|---|---|
| Mark Blackburn | Mayhem on Mackinac Island |
| Matt Sorenson | Dinosaurs Destroy Detroit |
| Tim Johnson | Mackinaw City Mummies |
| Nick and Summer | Terror Stalks Traverse City |
| Leah Warner | Poltergeists of Petoskey |
| Kayleigh Fisher | Aliens Attack Alpena |
| Kevin Barnes | Sinister Spiders of Saginaw |
| Corky and Ashley | Kreepy Klowns of Kalamazoo |
| Alex and Adrian | Strange Spirits of St. Ignace |
| Josh and Robyn | Gargoyles of Gaylord |

# About the author

Johnathan Rand is the author of the best-selling **'Chillers'** series, now with over 2,000,000 copies in print. In addition to the **'Chillers'** series, Rand is also the author of the **'Adventure Club'** series, including **'Ghost in the Graveyard'**, **'Ghost in the Grand'**, and **'The Haunted Schoolhouse'**, three collections of thrilling, original short stories. When Mr. Rand and his wife are not traveling to schools and book signings, they live in a small town in northern lower Michigan with their two dogs, Abby and Lily Munster. He is currently working on more 'Chillers', as well as a new series for younger readers entitled **'Freddie Fernortner, Fearless First Grader'**. His popular website features hundreds of photographs, stories, and art work. Visit:

## www.americanchillers.com

**Also by Johnathan Rand:**

# GHOST IN THE GRAVEYARD

Join the official

# AMERICAN CHILLERS

## FAN CLUB!

Visit www.americanchillers.com for details

**All AudioCraft books are proudly printed, bound, and manufactured in the United States of America, utilizing American resources, labor, and materials.**

# USA